D0646442

On Grandpa's Farm

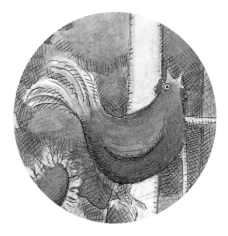

Vivian Sathre

Illustrated by Anne Hunter

Houghton Mifflin Company

Boston 1997

Text copyright © 1997 by Vivian Sathre
Illustrations copyright © 1997 by Anne Hunter

All rights reserved.
For information about permission to reproduce selections
from this book, write to Permissions, Houghton Mifflin Company,
215 Park Avenue South, New York, New York 10003.

For information about this and other Houghton Mifflin
trade and reference books and multimedia products,
visit The Bookstore at Houghton Mifflin
on the World Wide Web at http://www.hmco.com/trade/.

The text of this book is set in 24 point Granjon.
The illustrations are watercolor, pencil and ink, reproduced in full color.

Library of Congress Cataloging-in-Publication Data

Sathre, Vivian.
On Grandpa's farm / by Vivian Sathre; illustrated by Anne Hunter.
p. cm.
Summary: Simple text describes a day spent helping Grandpa with chores
on the farm.
ISBN 0-395-76506-4
[1. Farm life — Fiction. 2. Grandfathers — Fiction.]
I. Hunter, Anne, ill. II. Title.
PZ7.S249160n 1997
[E] — dc20 96-2995 CIP AC

Manufactured in the United States of America
WOZ 10 9 8 7 6 5 4 3 2 1

For Karsten and Alice Sathre,
the roots of love on Grandpa's farm.
—V.S.

For Kelsey.
—A.H.

Roosters crow.
Grandpa rises.

Oatmeal steams.
Fishing poles lean.

Queenie scampers.
Shadows stretch.

Cows munch.
Pigs push.

Chickens squabble.
Eggs hide.
I find.
Two drop.

Worms squirm.
Breezes whirl.

Scarecrow rustles.
Blackbirds scatter!

Pickets wiggle.
Grandpa holds.
I hammer.

Shadows hug.
Ice cubes clink.
Tackle box waits.

Tractor chugs.
Heat shimmers.
Baler bundles.
Hay drops.

Cows stray.
Queenie herds.
Grandpa milks.

Pigs root.
Chickens squawk.
Eggs nestle.
None drop!

Grandpa calls!

Lake ripples.
Bobbers dip.
Fish flop.

Shadows fade.
Fireflies flicker.

Supper sizzles.